Published 1985 by Derrydale Books, distributed by Crown Publishers, Inc.
© 1983 Editions Hemma
Text Copyright © 1985 Joshua Morris, Inc.
Printed in Belgium
h g f e d c b a

OSCAR
The Gardener

DERRYDALE BOOKS
New York

One bright spring day,
Oscar was hard at work in his garden.
"The sun is too hot," he said.
"I'll go inside and take a nap."
Soon, Oscar was fast asleep.

onions

door

chair

broom

basket

flower pot

watering can

"I'll help Oscar out in the garden," said Robbie.
"I can see he's working too hard!"

"I'll dig up the carrots," thought Robbie.
"Then Oscar will have room to plant something else."
Robbie put the carrots in his basket, and off he ran.

basket

carrots

hat

apron

shovel

"Oh, that Robbie! He must have dug up my carrots!" shouted Oscar.

tree

glass cover

butterfly

snail

"I know Robbie can't dig through these glass covers!" laughed Oscar. Soon all the carrots were growing safely under glass.

bicycle

basket

wheels

turtle

The next day, Robbie saw Oscar riding his bicycle.
"While Oscar's in town, I'll help dig up the rest of his garden," he said to himself.

**Robbie asked Mr. Mole and the little birds to help him.
"Won't Oscar be surprised when he sees all the work we've done!"**

"Robbie!" cried Oscar.
"How could you dig up all of my carrots?
Now, I have nothing to sell at the marketplace!"
Robbie felt terrible. "I was only trying to help," he said.
"I'll help you plant a new garden –
we'll plant flowers and grass too!"

larkspur

shovel

primrose

wheelbarrow

weathervane

ball

While Oscar started to work in the garden,
Robbie decided to play one more game of kickball.
Robbie kicked the ball very high.
"Oh no, now I've lost my brand-new ball," he cried.

turtle

greenhouse

plants

snail

watering can

Oscar planted his new flowers and vegetables very carefully.
"These new tomato plants are ready to go into the ground," he said.
"I'm glad I kept them in my greenhouse.
At least Robbie can't ruin any of my plants in there."

stakes

hammer

wheelbarrow

first aid kit

Oscar hammered wooden stakes into the
ground. "These poles are called stakes,"
Oscar told Robbie. "They'll help the
tomato plants to grow big and strong!"
But Robbie wasn't listening to Oscar.
He was watching out for his thumb!

tomato vine

turtle

hedgehog

seed bag

Next, Robbie planted grass seeds.
He did just what Oscar told him to do.
And he scattered them all over the ground.
Oscar was having trouble with Mr. Mole.
"Can't you find a new home, Mr. Mole!" cried Oscar.

mole hill

mole

roller

I'm doing my best to do a good job for Oscar," said Robbie. "Working in the garden is fun and easy!"

Suddenly Oscar cried out,
"Hey! What happened to the water?"
"Oh look, my new hat is ruined!" cried Kitty.
"I think you both need more lessons
in the garden!"

sunflower

hat

hose

snail

fence

"Kitty is right," said Oscar.
"There's more to gardening,
than just fun and play."

dig   rake   punch holes   hoe

"Look at our vegetables!" said Robbie.
"I think Oscar and I know how to grow a garden now."

field

Robbie helped to gather all the vegetables.
"Whew! This pumpkin is as big as I am!" he exclaimed.

water

pumpkin

"Oh, Oscar! I just found this new home!" cried little mouse.

bushel basket

truck

potatoes

pumpkin

artichoke

lettuce

cauliflower

carrots

asparagus

onions

Soon everything was loaded in the truck
and ready to be taken to the market.
"Oscar, stop! Slow Down!
Oh well, I'm sure we'll have plenty to sell
at the market next year!"